A long time ago, there lived a man called Stan Bolovan. He and his wife had a good life, but they had no children and this made the wife sad. She cried and cried, which made Stan sad, too.

One morning, Stan met a wise man.

“My wife and I wish we had children, but we do not,” he said.

The wise man said, “Are you rich? Can you feed children if you have them?”

“If we can have children, we will feed them,” said Stan.

When Stan got back home, there were children everywhere. There were some in the garden, some in the house, and even some up a tree! In the middle of all of the noisy children, Stan's wife sat and smiled.

When Stan found out that the hundred children were his, he was shocked.

"Goodness!" he said. "What a lot of children!"

Within a couple of weeks, the big family had run out of food.

"I must go and get some food from somewhere," said Stan, and off he went.

A long while later, Stan came to the end of the Earth.

When he got there, it was dark. Stan found a big flock of sheep. He huddled up with them to go to sleep.

Some time later, Stan heard a loud whoosh. It was a dragon! The dragon stole some of the sheep.

In the morning, Stan went to the shepherd.

"What will you give me if I get rid of this terrible dragon?"

"I will give you seventy sheep's cheeses," said the shepherd, giving Stan a big round cheese.

"I can feed all of my children with these!" said Stan.

That evening, Stan hid by the sheep again. A loud whoosh told him that the dragon had landed next to him. Stan was terrified, but he needed to feed his children so he stood still.

"Who are you?" shouted the dragon.

Stan pretended to be a strongman. "I am Stan Bolovan," he said. "I can crush rocks in my teeth, and I will stop you carrying off more of these sheep."

The dragon was afraid of Stan.

“I am so strong that I can squeeze buttermilk out of a rock,” said Stan. With that, he picked up the big cheese (which looked like a rock), and squeezed the buttermilk out of it.

The dragon fell for Stan’s trick.

Despite being afraid of Stan, the dragon said, "My wife and I need a strongman like you to help us with chores. If you come with me for one week, I will give you seven sacks of gold coins."

Stan went with the dragon.

"I can buy food to feed all of my children with those coins," he said to himself.

The dragon's wife told Stan to fetch wood from the forest. When he got there, Stan started to tie all of the trees in the forest together.

"What are you doing?" said the dragon.

“If I tie the trees together and then tug on this rope, I can uproot all of the trees at the same time,” said Stan.

You cannot uproot the whole forest!” the dragon shouted. “Here, let me fetch the wood for you.”

The whole week went on like this. Every time Stan was given a chore to do, he tricked the dragon into doing it for him! Before long, the week was up. The dragon was happy to be getting rid of Stan.

The dragon carried the sacks of gold to Stan's house. When they arrived, Stan's hungry children came rushing out with knives and forks.

"Lunch!" they shouted.

The terrified dragon fled.

The dragon and his wife were never seen again. The shepherd was so grateful that he paid Stan the seventy sheep's cheeses. With those and the sacks of gold coins, Stan and his family never went hungry again!